80-14268

PSS

5

13

6

D1558485

Also by Michael Scheier and Julie Frankel:
THE WHOLE MIRTH CATALOG

WHAT TO DO with THE ROCKS IN YOUR HEAD

AN ACTIVITY BOOK WITH A SENSE OF HUMOR

THINGS TO MAKE AND DO ALONE, WITH FRIENDS, WITH FAMILY, INSIDE AND OUTSIDE

MICHAEL

JULIE

SCHEIER & FRANKEL

A GROLIER COMPANY

FRANKLIN WATTS
NEW YORK/LONDON/TORONTO/SYDNEY
1980

Library of Congress Cataloging in Publication Data

Scheier, Michael.
What to do with the rocks in your head.

SUMMARY: Suggestions for a variety of
unusual activities, games, and crafts.
1.   Games—Juvenile literature.
2.   Amusements—Juvenile literature.
3.   Creative activities and seat work—
Juvenile literature. [1. Games. 2. Handicraft]
I.   Frankel, Julie, joint author.
II.   Title.
GV1203.S394   790.1   80–14268
ISBN 0–531–04174–3

Special thanks to
Jennifer, Jennifer, and Allison

·CONTENTS·

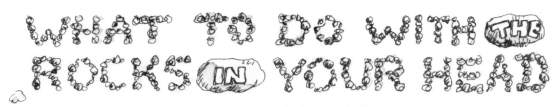

WHAT TO DO WITH THE ROCKS IN YOUR HEAD

DUMMY!

POISON IVY

DO IT OUTSIDE

DISGUISE'S THE LIMIT

DO IT INSIDE

Sensationals

ICE CREAM BOTTOMS UP

On a hot summer day,
buy ice cream cones with your friends.

Bite the bottoms off all at the same time.
Suck the ice cream from the bottom.

First person to eat all the ice cream
from the bottom wins!

Have napkins in your pocket; you may need them.

SLURP!

Put pudding or yogurt in shallow dishes.
See who can eat it all first.
(No hands allowed.)

THE GREAT BLINDFOLDED TASTING CONTEST

Do you really know the difference between Brand X and Brand Y?
Can you pick your favorite foods?
Blindfold two or more people.
Give them each two or three brands of the same product to taste.

Use as many different things as you have time and budget for.

peanut butter   cola   orange juice

bread   yogurt   chocolate ice cream

potato chips   margarine vs. butter

low fat milk vs. whole milk   ice milk vs. ice cream

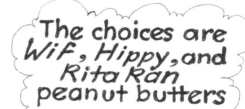

The choices are Wif, Hippy, and Rita Ran peanut butters

As you feed each person a taste, announce the choices.

Keep an accurate list of each person and each product.

RIGHT ANSWERS →	PEANUT BUTTER			
	Wif 1	Hippy 2	Rita Ran 3	
Allison	2	1	3	
Jennifer	1	3	2	
Bobbie	2	2	2	

Be careful not to mix up products; tasters can get very excited.
At the end of each tasting, announce the answers and the person who most often guessed correctly.

BODY TALK

Bodies are machines that are always on. Tune them in.

Listen to someone's heart beating.

Listen to a friend's empty stomach,
then listen after a meal.

Put a cracker or a bite of bread
on your tongue; try not to salivate.
Challenge your friend.

Count how many times you swallow
in a minute, in five minutes, in an hour.

Count how many times you blink
in a minute, in five minutes, in an hour.

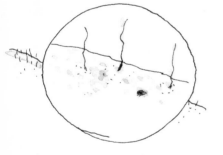

Look at your skin through a magnifying
glass. Look for hair, lines, freckles.

See how many people you know who can:

    wiggle their ears,
    touch their nose with their tongue,
    curl their tongue, and
    flop it on its side,
    touch their thumb to their wrist,
    have a second toe longer than their big toe.

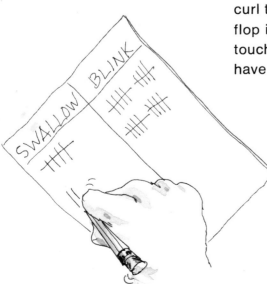

MIND WALK

Take a walk with your mind.

Sit yourself down in a familiar part of the house.

> In your mind,
> get up out of the chair,
> walk to the closet,
> and put on your coat.

Imagine yourself opening the door
and going outside.

Take a walk; go wherever you want.

> Try to see in your mind
> all that you would be seeing
> if you were really walking.

Turn around.

Come home a different way in your mind.

> Come in the door.
> Walk to your chair.
> Sit down.

> Now get up for real.

> Go out and see
> if you saw
> all there is to see.

Get permission to make your room into a

CHAMBER OF HORRORS!

This will be a dark environment you will lead your friends through.

Transform the room in as many ways as you can think of.

Put sheets over the furniture. Tape on ghost eyeholes and other scaries.

Cut bats out of black paper and hang them up.

Hang up lots of spider webs. Make the webs by tying long lengths of sewing thread onto string or yarn. Hang them all over the room.

Record a cassette of weird sounds, cackles, and creepy music to play when you lead people through.

Plan your own costume to go with the room. Turn off the lights, pull the shades and shine a flashlight under your chin for the eeriest look.

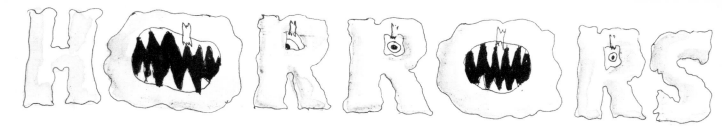

Prepare Boogey Bowls.

Bowl of Eyeballs

peel 30 grapes
or fill bowl with
olives

Bag of Guts

fill plastic bag with
cooked spaghetti or macaroni

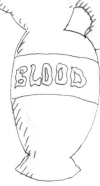

Platter of Fingers

pile cooked carrots or
small pickles on plate

Blood Drink

mix cranberry and
grape juice or
use your favorite
red juice (looks
scary when lit
from bottom with
small flashlight)

Witches' Hearts

chilled stewed prunes
or plums

Bat Brains

bowl of mashed
potatoes

Set up tables or other flat surfaces throughout the chamber.

Just before the tours begin, set out the Boogey Bowls.

Have your friends wash their hands.

Lead them through and have them feel these guckies, while explaining that they are touching eyeballs, guts, etc.

If you can't get your chamber dark enough, blindfold your guests before they enter.

Have each person become a creature in the environment after you have led them through it.

Afterwards have a picnic with all the food.

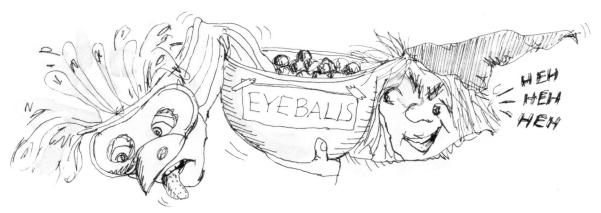

FUNNY FOOD COMBOS

BANANA DOGS

Peel a banana.
Place it in a hot dog roll.
Smear banana with peanut butter, instead of mustard.
Chomp.

MASHED POTATO MUNDAE

Use an ice cream scoop
to put a couple of mashed potato balls
into a Mundae dish.
A hollowed out green pepper is a Mundae dish.
Spoon on gravy.
Top with a cherry tomato or an olive.

To make a C and C split,
stick long slices of carrots and cucumbers
into the sides of the Mashed Potato Mundae.

Eat it with an edible spoon.
Edible spoons are celery stalks.

When you have finished the Mundae,
eat the Mundae dish.
Eat the edible spoon.
Eat . . .

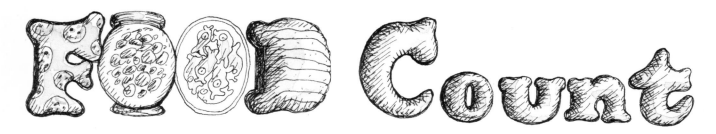

FOOD Count

Guess:

how many olives in a jar?

how many sardines in a can?

how many sections in a tangerine?

how many candies in a box?

how many potatoes in a sack?

how many slices of bread in a loaf?

how many cookies in a bag?

how many slices of bacon in a package?

SENSATIONALS

Don't talk for a day; carry a pad, and communicate only by writing or sign language.

Use the hand you usually don't write with. Try getting dressed, eating, writing, and doing everything, with your opposite hand.

Put on a clean pair of gloves or mittens when you get up. Brush your teeth and your hair, have breakfast, and wear them all day.

Talk with your hands over both ears. Talk with your hand over one ear.

Without using your hands, close one eyelid at a time.

Arch one eyebrow at a time.

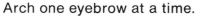

Put on a blindfold. Have a friend hand you objects. By simply feeling them, try to *see* what they are.

At night lie quietly in your bed; listen hard; try to identify each sound.

FLOWER

I.

On a nice day,
find a flower you want to know better; sit down beside it.
Watch it for a while.
Get closer and closer to it.
You will start to notice colors, shapes, parts you never saw.
Use a magnifying glass to look even closer.

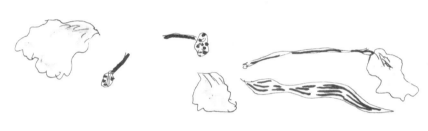

II.

To see even more than before, pick the flower.
Slowly and carefully use a tweezers to take it apart.
Use the magnifying glass to examine the flower's parts
as you dissect it.
When you have finished,
find another flower just like the one you have dissected.
Look at it.
How does it look now?

III.

Go to a library or bookstore and get a book about flowers.
Go further inside the flower by learning the names of the parts,
and how to identify flowers that grow where you live.

eye TALK

Sit down in a comfortable spot with a friend.
Look into each other's eyes. Keep staring.
Look for yourself in the other person's eyes.
Tell each other what you are seeing.
Look at the colors, and patterns, and speckles.
See if you can talk with your eyes.

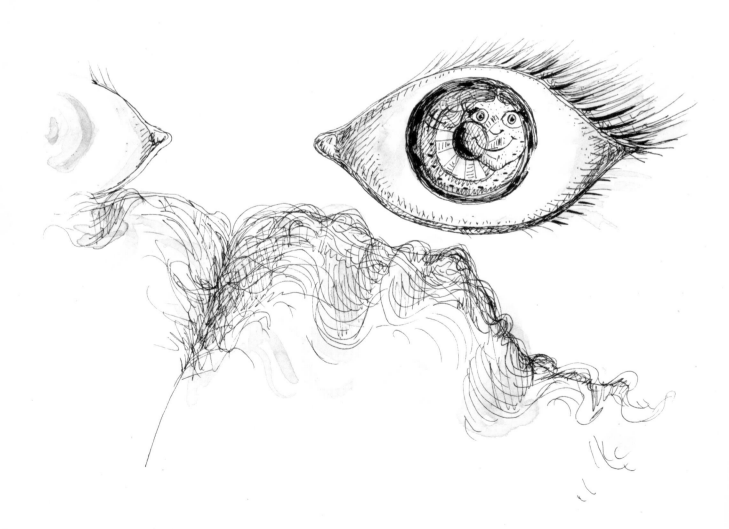

RECALL ROOM

Have a friend close his or her eyes.
Walk with your friend to a familiar part of the house.
Name the room you have picked.
Have your friend name everything he or she can think of
in the room.

Ask:

    what colors things are,
    how many books are on a shelf, and their titles,
    what kinds of plants are on the sill,
    what the labels on the jars say,
    what clothes are lying around,
    what the pictures on the wall look like,
    what games are in the chest, and so on.

When you're both tired, have your friend open his or her eyes
to see how well he or she has really seen.

Switch places.
Close your eyes.
Have your friend walk *you* to a familiar part of the house.

CAN YOU

With your *eyes closed* can you:

Write your name between two lines on notebook paper,

draw a smiling face,

draw a person?

Can you live for just one day, one week, one month,

without TV?

without RADIO?

without STEREO?

without CANDY?

without COMICS?

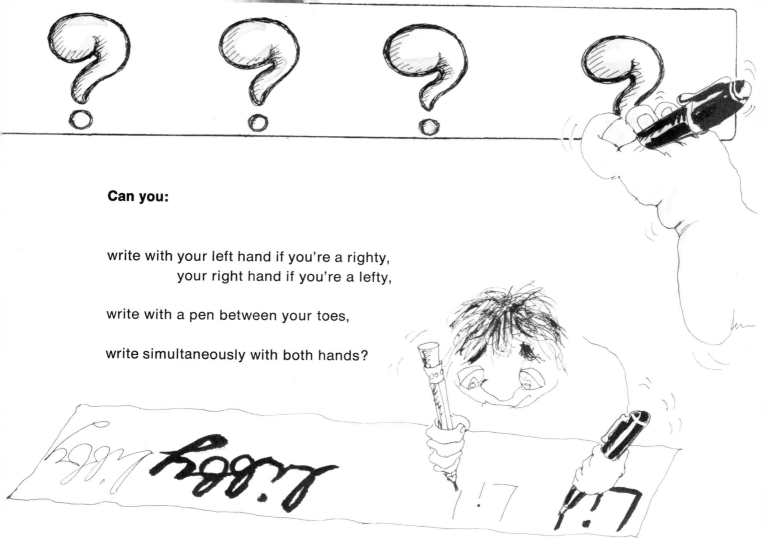

Can you:

write with your left hand if you're a righty,
your right hand if you're a lefty,

write with a pen between your toes,

write simultaneously with both hands?

Can you live for just one day, one week, one month,

without TELEPHONE?

without MUSIC?

without FAST FOOD?

PROVE IT!!!

BATS

Play in a large open space, free of obstacles.

One person makes a continuous noise. The rest of the players have their eyes covered, and must slowly home in on the sound. Try BATS from 10 feet (2.7 m) away.

BEEP BEEP BEEP BEEP BEEP

MEATLOAF CLAY

You will need:

chopped meat
bread crumbs
egg(s)
milk
a teaspoon of oil
or a pat of butter
a large bowl
a plate
a spatula
a pan

Meatloaf Clay Recipe

For every pound (.45 kg) of chopped meat,
add one egg and one cup of bread crumbs.

With clean hands, mix chopped meat, egg,
and bread crumbs in a large bowl.
Mush it up until it is totally mixed.

If it's too wet or sticky, add a few
crumbs. If it's too dry add
a few drops of milk.

optional decorations:

ketchup, cheese, tomato, onion, peppers,
bacon, celery, carrots, mustard

Spread the oil all over the pan to prevent sticking.

Have the oven preheated to 350°F (175°C).

Roll the clay into balls and make
whatever you want: a large face,
a person, a heart, a star.

Use your decorations to add:
eyes, noses, mouths, dots, horns.

Put your works of art on the pan.
Cook 1 inch (2.5 cm) thick sculptures
    15 minutes for rare,
    20 minutes for well done.

Eat and enjoy!

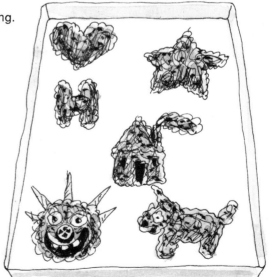

At a party, give each guest his or her own ball of meatloaf clay, and a greased
sheet of aluminum foil to work on. Set out a large platter of decorations. Have your
mother or father collect all the sculptures, cook them, and serve them for lunch.

WATCHIN'

Get a good seat outside,

a rock you like,
a bench you know,
a tree for your back,
or that private place you go.

Relax.
Watch the leaves fall to the ground.
Which trees are losing more leaves?
Which leaf will blow off next?

Later,
find a comfy seat inside.
Watch the rain fall or
the snow.
Watch it build up until it sticks.
Follow a snowflake
or a raindrop
until it hits the ground.

Dawn's Early Light

Find out from the newspaper, radio, or weather bureau exactly what time the sun is going to rise.
Find out which window will have the best view.

Set your alarm for ten minutes before sunrise.

Watch!

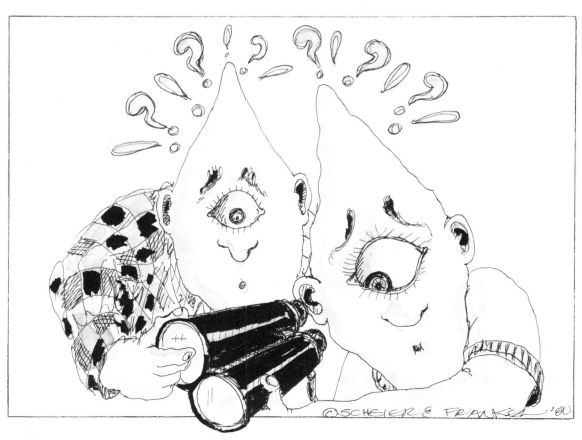

GURGLE
THE INCREDIBLE SOUND TEST

Use a cassette recorder to tape ten different sounds you hear every day:

refrigerator opening   toilet flushing
can being opened   doorbell   vacuum cleaner
cat meowing   phone being dialed   gargling
clapping   eating potato chips

Assign a number to each sound and announce it as you record the sound. Keep an answer sheet for yourself with the number and name of each sound.

Let the recorder run for a few seconds between each sound, then shut it off.

Hand out pencils and paper to your family or friends. Have them try to identify the sounds.

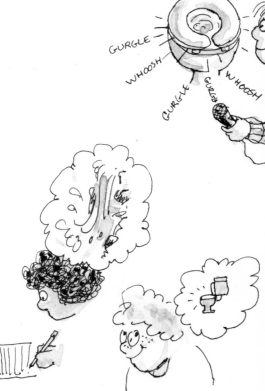

WHAT TO DO WITH THE ROCKS IN YOUR HEAD

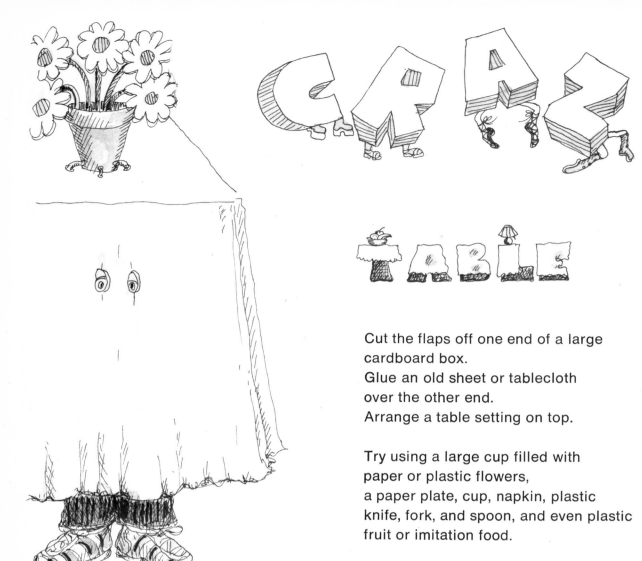

CRAZY TABLE

Cut the flaps off one end of a large
cardboard box.
Glue an old sheet or tablecloth
over the other end.
Arrange a table setting on top.

Try using a large cup filled with
paper or plastic flowers,
a paper plate, cup, napkin, plastic
knife, fork, and spoon, and even plastic
fruit or imitation food.

Glue the whole setting down.
Let it dry.
Cut two eyeholes after you've tried on
your table.
Wear brown pants or make cardboard legs.

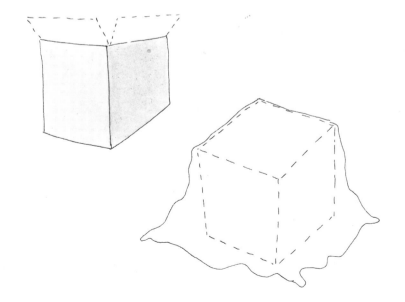

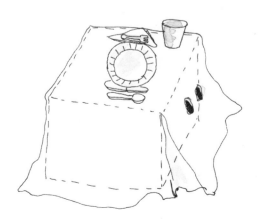

COSTUMES

WASHING MACHINE

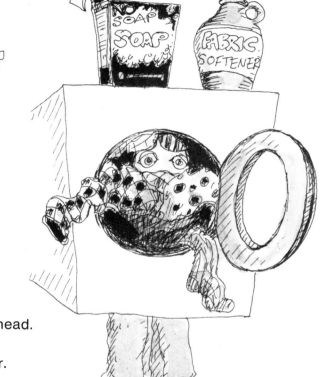

Get a large box you can fit in.
Draw a large circle on one side.
Cut open ¾ of the circle.
This will be the door.

Draw a handle on the outside
of the door.
Draw dials on top of the machine.
Glue empty soap containers on top.

Put an old shirt with eyeholes cut out over your head.
Wrap your body in a sheet.
Hang some old clothes over the edge of the door.
Attach them with clothespins.
Get inside.

APARTMENT COMPLEX

Glue boxes of different sizes and shapes together on top of a large box you can fit in.

Paint the boxes different colors, or one color.

Draw small bricks over the entire costume.

Draw on or cut out windows and doors.

Add on small people and pets, trees, and bushes.

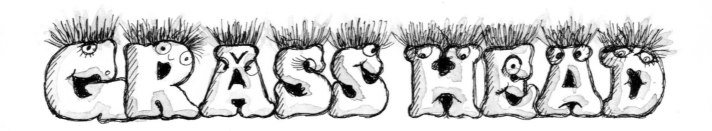

GRASS HEAD

You'll need: a waxed or styrofoam cup
a cupful of soil
a handful of pebbles
a spoonful of grass seed

Draw or paint a face on the cup.

If the cup has a pattern on it, cover it with plain paper, then draw on a face.

Line the bottom of the cup with pebbles.

Fill with soil almost to the top.

Drop in the seeds.
Cover the seeds with soil.
Water.
Place near a window.

Water again in a few days when the soil is dry.

In about a week GRASSHEAD will start to grow hair.

Turn the cup every few days so the grass grows evenly.

Trim with a scissors when and how you want.

The Pits

Pit one pit against the other.

Line two pots with gravel, add soil,
and plant an avocado pit in each pot.

Cover with soil.
Water when dry.
See which comes up first
or grows the highest.

Try racing grapefruit seeds.

EGG PLANT

AMAZING MAZES

How to Make a Maze

Start with one canal.
Make it straight, angled, or wavy.

Make two branches.
Make one of those branches a dead end.

Make two or more branches.
Make all but one into a dead end.
Always keep track of your path.
Always leave a way out.

Keep going until you've filled a page.

Make carbon or photocopies and give as gifts.

Draw a shape; it could be abstract or real.
Leave "in" and "out" openings.
Fill the shape with a maze.

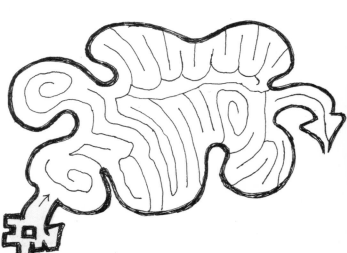

IN ONE EAR...
AND OUT THE OTHER!

COLLECTOR

Start a unique collection.

Not stamps, trading cards, or dolls.
   Be different.
   Collect something you like.
   Collect everything about it.
   Collect:
      Frisbees,
      candy wrappers,
      T-shirts,
      fast-food paraphernalia,
      articles, pictures, and
      products of a famous person.
   Read up on your collection.
   Become an expert.

FRED'S IV COMMANDMENTS

Flatten a piece of clay.
Make two holes at the top.

Use a pencil to imprint
your own commandments.

Let your tablet dry,
and hang it outside your room.

DO NOT ENTER WITHOUT KNOCKING

NO PARENTS!

THOU SHALT NOT BOTHER A PERSON LISTENING TO MUSIC

BE NICE TO YOUR CHILD

What to do with the rocks in your head... build a miniature stone castle ? ?

Collect a bunch of small rocks, stones, and pebbles.

Build a small house, a castle with many turrets, a fort, a mansion for dolls, or a whole village.

Spread out plenty of newspaper. A wooden board is a good surface to build castles on. Draw an outline on the board first.

Glue the stones together with white glue, or use a mixture that looks like real mortar.

Mortar Mix

3 parts flour
2 parts sand
2 parts water
3 parts white glue

Mix the dry ingredients in an old can or dish. Add glue and water, and stir until the whole thing is a sticky glob, like toothpaste. If it's too wet and runny, add tiny bits of flour until it's stiff enough. If it's too stiff, add a few drops of water.

Goop a spoonful of mortar mix onto the board; smear it over the outline of your first wall. Place the stones in the mortar mix. For the second layer, "butter" each rock by using a Popsicle stick to scoop up enough mortar mix to cover the bottom and sides of each new rock. Press the buttered rocks gently into place. Use smaller stones to fill big spaces between larger rocks. Let each layer dry before adding more stones.

What Makes It Tick?

Ask for an old clock, watch, or
even an old typewriter
that no longer works.

Ask to take it apart.
Study the pieces.
Arrange them in groups that you like.

Glue them to a nice wooden board
and display it.

FATHER TIME

Make up a list of things you do often.

Guess how long it takes to:
- brush your teeth
- comb your hair
- eat breakfast, lunch, dinner
- blow a bubble
- tie your shoes
- take a bath

Write down your estimates.

	ME	MOM	DAD
Toothbrushing			
hair combing			
breakfast			
lunch			
dinner			
bubble blowing			
shoe tying			
bathing			

Now time yourself as you do these things.
Were you close?

Try timing other people.

Decide what you want to draw.

Mix drawing and typing.

Type slowly and carefully.

JUDIE'S WORST PERSON of the Month!

Mr. Shyerv, the Grouch!

Decide for your very own personal reasons who is the WORST PERSON OF THE MONTH.

Put a photo or drawing of that person in an old frame.

Hang it!

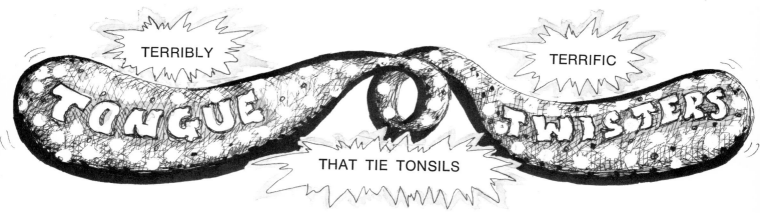

TERRIBLY

TONGUE

THAT TIE TONSILS

TERRIFIC

TWISTERS

Write your own tongue twister.
Choose five or ten words that start with the same letter.
Put them together to make a funny phrase or sentence.
Use the dictionary for more complicated twisters.
Say it fast three times, five times, ten times!

Make one for someone you like, using the first letter of that friend's name.

Marvelous, magical Marge, methodically munching morel mushrooms, makes mental miracles multiply!

TREASURIUM

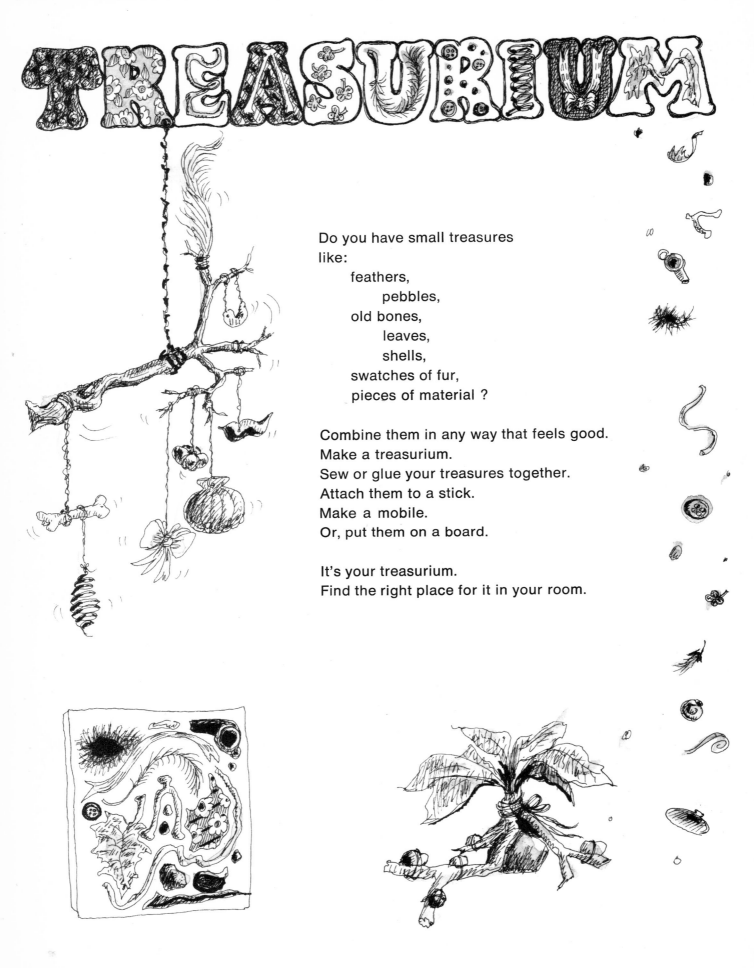

Do you have small treasures
like:
      feathers,
         pebbles,
    old bones,
       leaves,
       shells,
  swatches of fur,
  pieces of material ?

Combine them in any way that feels good.
Make a treasurium.
Sew or glue your treasures together.
Attach them to a stick.
Make a mobile.
Or, put them on a board.

It's your treasurium.
Find the right place for it in your room.

PUZZLING

The easiest puzzle to make is from a favorite drawing, poster, or photo.

Paste this onto cardboard, or draw directly on the cardboard.

When dry, sketch the outline of the pieces on the back.

Cut them out.

Puzzle pieces don't have to look like:

The shape of your puzzle doesn't have to be:

It can be:

When you have finished, take a picture of the puzzle. Paste it onto a box or can with a top. Put the pieces inside.

For a sturdier puzzle, use masonite. Either glue a picture or paint directly on it. Cut out the pieces with a coping saw.

For your first puzzle, try to keep the pieces large.

TIME CAPSULE

Send a Time Capsule into your future.

Before the year ends, perhaps on your winter vacation,
prepare a box, large jar, or scrapbook that will
show what you, your year, and the world have been like.

Put in pictures, the front page of a newspaper,
advertisements for products or shows that you like,
small objects, things you've collected, your
autobiography, a message to the future.

Seal your Time Capsule; put it in a safe place!

Make one each year.

Keep them forever.

Open them when
you want to look
back on where and
what you've been.

Make your own calendar.
Use a calendar for the coming year as a guide.
Decide what you want on your calendar. It can be anything.
You can draw on small pictures, or make up your own holidays.

Holidays you might want to use:
    family birthdays
        birthdays of anyone you think is important
            your own undays (see page 48) and unweeks
                silly holidays
                    great moments in your life

THIS IS YOUR LIFE!

A movie of your life is being made!

Who is playing you and everyone important to you?
What do the sets look like?
What are some of the major events?
If the movie takes place in the future,
who is starring as your husband, wife, or children?

Make a poster advertising the movie.

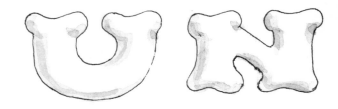

IT'S A S-L-O-O-O-W DAY

From the moment you wake up, do everything in slow motion.
Wash, get dressed, and eat in slow motion.
Stage a slow motion fight. Have a slow motion chase.
Talk in s-l-o-o-o-w m-o-o-o-t-i-o-n.
Walk in s-l-o-o-o-w m-o-o-o-t-i-o-n.
Will you drive yourself or your family crazy first?

HAVE AN UNBIRTHDAY

Get your parents to give you one, or give them one,
or surprise your brother or sister.
There are no rules.
(Surprises are nice.)

Every day is wonderful. It does not have to be your birthday
for you to be happy you were born.

DAYS

THROUGH THE LOOKING GLASS DAY

Do everything opposite or backwards; it's your choice!

When you wake up, put at least one piece of clothing on backwards
or inside out.
Say yes when you mean no.
Try eating an inside-out sandwich: put a slice of bread between
two pieces of meat or cheese.
Have breakfast for dinner.
Get permission to take a bath with some of your clothes on.
Use your imagination.
!NUF EVAH

OTHER UNDAYS

Kid's Day
Pet's Birthday
First Day of Summer Vacation
Eat What You Want Day

Add your favorite undays
to your calendar (see page 45).

Make up your own word
or use an old one in a new way.

Put your word in circulation.
Say it whenever you can.
Write it in letters.
Get your friends to use it.

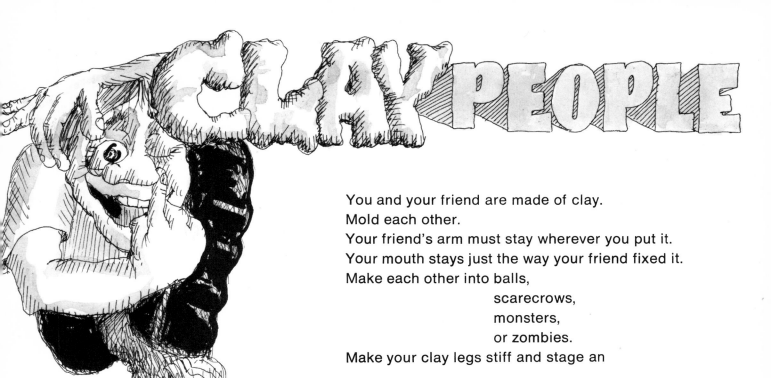

THE CLAY PEOPLE

You and your friend are made of clay.
Mold each other.
Your friend's arm must stay wherever you put it.
Your mouth stays just the way your friend fixed it.
Make each other into balls,
                  scarecrows,
                  monsters,
                  or zombies.
Make your clay legs stiff and stage an

ATTACK
OF
THE
CLAY PEOPLE

There is only one rule: don't hurt the other person.
Never push an arm, or leg, or any body part where it won't go.

AGE TAG

BABIES!

You are it.
Call out one age or one time of life.
Try:

fetuses in the womb
        infants
    two-year-olds
right now
        teenagers
    twenty-one
middle aged
        old
    two-hundred-years-old

While you are chasing everyone, you and
they must act out the age or time
of life that you have called out.

The person you tag is It and calls out
a different age or time of life.

Play until exhausted.

You're it!

OLD!

OOOOH...
my arthritis!

PRETEND....

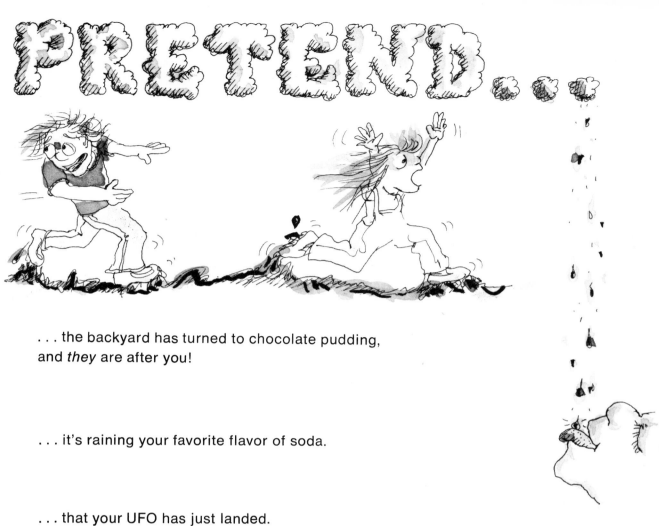

. . . the backyard has turned to chocolate pudding,
and *they* are after you!

. . . it's raining your favorite flavor of soda.

. . . that your UFO has just landed.
What will you say to the earthlings?
Are you afraid of them?
Are they afraid of you?
What special powers do you have?
What weaknesses?

. . . you are Zotz!, super-hero extraordinaire,
and you are about to tangle with
a three-tailed fenopede.

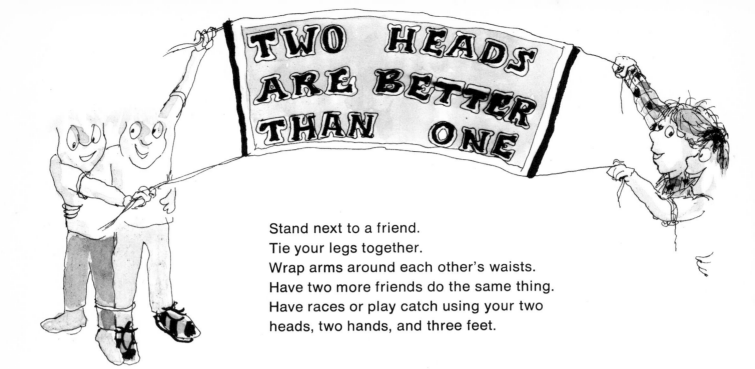

Stand next to a friend.
Tie your legs together.
Wrap arms around each other's waists.
Have two more friends do the same thing.
Have races or play catch using your two
heads, two hands, and three feet.

Sit down back to back. Link arms at the elbow.
Try to stand up.
Race another couple to see who can stand first.

beetle twins

Spread your legs. Bend down. Put your hands
between your legs and link hands with your twin,
backside to backside.
Hop, scurry, run, waddle, or race another pair
of beetle twins.

LOCAL RECORD BOOK

Set your own records with your friends.

How long, and how many times can you:
volley a tennis, Ping-Pong,
or volleyball?
jump a rope?
stay on a roller coaster?
throw a Frisbee?
hop on one foot?

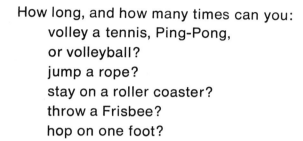

How high can you stack:
checkers?
cards?
dominoes?
pennies?

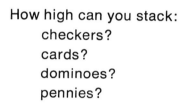

How far can you:
walk with a book on your head?
blow a soap bubble?

Make your own book of local records.

SECRETS

Keep a secret
by yourself or
with a friend.
Do not ever tell anyone else.

Do something nice for someone.
Keep it a secret.
Leave flowers,
    send a card,
        leave a special present,
            or do a favor.
Keep it between you and you.
Give yourself the Golden Halo Award.

Snake Eyes

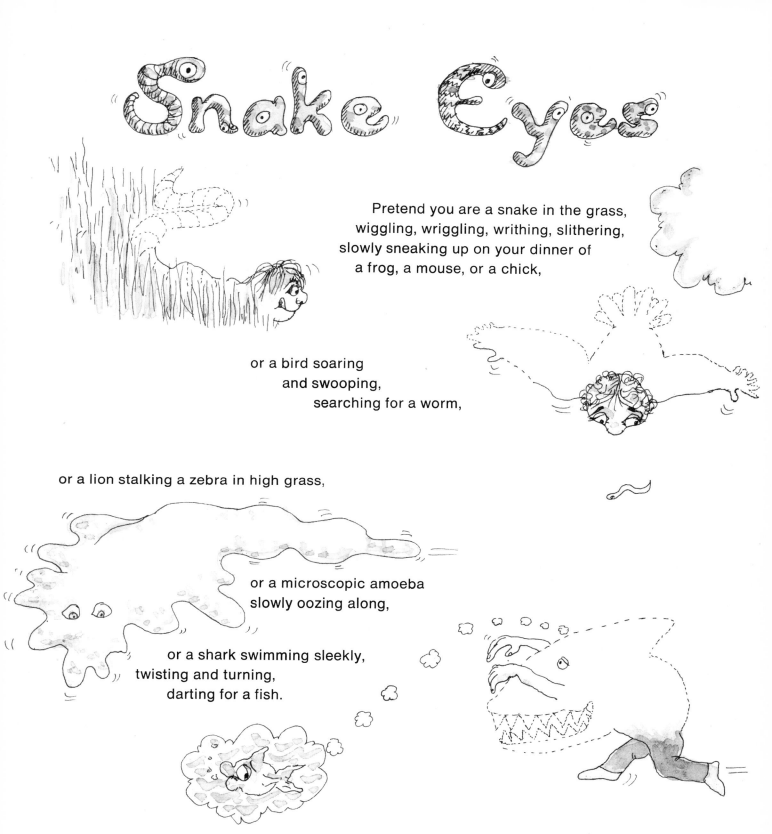

Pretend you are a snake in the grass,
wiggling, wriggling, writhing, slithering,
slowly sneaking up on your dinner of
a frog, a mouse, or a chick,

or a bird soaring
and swooping,
searching for a worm,

or a lion stalking a zebra in high grass,

or a microscopic amoeba
slowly oozing along,

or a shark swimming sleekly,
twisting and turning,
darting for a fish.

SNAKE EYES can be played alone, or with a friend.
Change places and switch parts.

DUMMY!

Be a ventriloquist; your friend is the dummy!

EASY DUMMY

Have your friend sit on your knee. Put your hand behind the dummy's head. Carry on a conversation. You act like a ventriloquist; your friend acts and talks like a dummy.

HARD DUMMY

Put your friend on your knee; place your hand behind the dummy's neck. Have the dummy open its mouth every time you press its neck. Talk for both of you. Try not to move your mouth when you are speaking for the dummy.

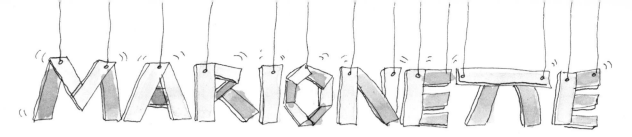

MARIONETTE

Cut four lengths of string or yarn
each 6 feet (1.8 m) long.

Sit a friend down on the floor.
Tie a string to his or her hands and feet.
Your friend has become a marionette.

The marionette should become limp.
Pull the strings.
Lift an arm. Flop it over the marionette's shoulder.
Lift a leg. Cross it over the other leg.

(It's okay to tell the marionette
what to do while you're moving the strings.)
The marionette can also put on marionette makeup.

MIME

Have an imaginary tug-of-war.
Lean on an imaginary shelf.
Press up against an imaginary window.

Move like a robot. Make a robot sound
over and over. Suffer a power shortage
and wind down.

Make up your own pantomimes.
Practice in front of a mirror.
Try your routines out on your family and friends.

CATCH! Egg Ball!

Carefully,
crack an egg open.
Cook and eat it.
Carefully put the shell halves
together again.

Use glue, if the shells don't
hold together.

When it is dry,
toss it to an unsuspecting friend
who has both hands free.
Your friend will be surprised,
but probably will catch it.

If you have more than one egg ball,
keep them in an empty egg carton.

HOLIDAY CUTUPS

Lay out all your old holiday cards, wrapping paper, ribbons, and cancelled stamps.

Cut out the parts you like; make a scene or a design.
Paste your favorites down on cardboard or paper.
Put it up on your wall or store it in your
Time Capsule (see page 44).

Feeling Good...

Get together with your friends and rehearse eight songs. Make an appointment to sing them for the people in a nearby nursing home.

Gather your toys that you don't play with anymore, and ask your parent to donate them to a hospital or day-care center.

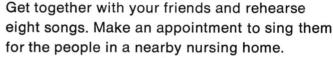

Send holiday cards to people in hospitals.

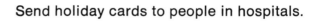

Put on a puppet show for the younger kids in the children's wing of a hospital.

Make up special awards for all the nice people you know and mail them.

BUG EYES

Look at the ground.
Find an ant, caterpillar, or other bug.
Follow it.
Follow it until it goes where you can't go.

Watch for:

spiders waiting for dinner,

crawlies going back and forth
to a food source,

bugs dragging other dead bugs
home to eat them,

burying beetles digging holes
to bury small dead animals.

Roll-the-Roll

Stage the Great International Toilet Paper Race!

Use one roll of toilet paper and an empty paper-towel roll for each racer.

Set up for the race by
     unrolling each roll of toilet paper
     in an open space or
     around your house.

Now race!

The first person to roll up
all the toilet paper onto a
towel roll wins.

If the paper should break,
the racer picks up the loose end
and continues on.

*(Recycle the paper. Use it to
make a mummy. See page 78.)

DON'T LITTER!*

HOT WEATHER WATER WARS

Fill a balloon with water
and tie it closed.

Stand opposite your opponent.
Toss the balloon back and forth.
Move farther apart.
Keep tossing.
Move still farther apart.
Game ends when one person gets a bath.

Repeat to see how far apart you can get.

SQUEEZE WAR

Rinse out plastic squeeze bottles.
Soap and hand lotion containers work well.

Change into bathing suits. Fill the
squeeze bottles with water. Arm each person
with the same number of bottles.

Set up buckets of water in
neutral territory for refilling.

Squeeze until drenched.

SIDEWALK ART MUSEUM

Ask permission to use a concrete area for chalk drawing.

Pretend the cement is a wall in the world's best museum,
and that you and your friends are the world's finest artists.

First draw yourself a gorgeous frame.
Put your masterpiece inside the frame.
Hold an exhibit.
Take pictures of your pictures.

SNOW SHUFFLING

With a few friends
make a circular path in the snow.

Walk it a few times with your eyes open
to get a feel for how much turning is involved.

With your eyes closed or blindfolded,
take turns trying to walk this circle back to the beginning
without stepping out of it.

You might be able to feel the boundaries of the circle
with the side of your foot, if you're careful.

Try more complicated figures,
a figure eight, a zigzag,
or a squiggle.

Fill milk cartons and other used waxy or plastic food containers with water. (DON'T use glass!)

Add food coloring.

Leaves, pine needles, and other natural objects will freeze beautifully if added to the water.

Place the containers outside to freeze.
When they are frozen solid, run the containers under warm water to slide the ice out.

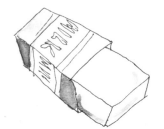

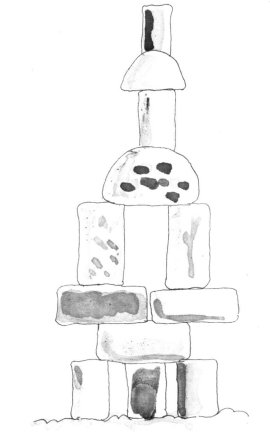

Take the Rainbow Ice Bricks outside and build a pyramid, a wall, or a sculpture.

(Always wear gloves.)

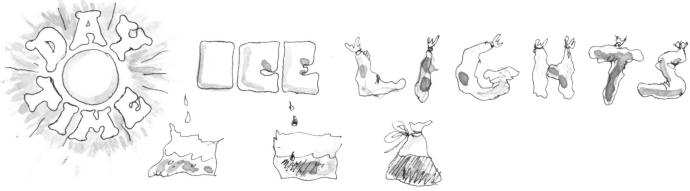

Fill clear plastic sandwich bags halfway with water. Add food coloring. Twist tops closed and tie with rubber bands. Hang the bags from a bush or tree. Hang them from branches that are strong and won't bend too much. The liquid will freeze and thaw as the temperature goes down and up.

POISON IVY

One person is the Poison Ivy monster and chases the group until it catches someone. It attaches one of its vine-arms to his or her waist. This person becomes part of the monster, which now reaches out with three vine-arms for new victims.

No one can escape becoming part of the monster—eventually!

PAPER AIRPLANE COMPETITION

Settle it once and for all!
Whose plane can go the farthest?
does the most loops?
goes the highest?
stays in the air the longest?

Fly the planes on level ground.
Fly them from a hill.

LEAF-LYMPICS

With your friends, gather the largest bunch of leaves you possibly can. The more the better. Do it in your yard or in a field, but NEVER in the street.

PILE JUMPING — Build the leaves as high as possible. Take turns jumping over and into the pile.

Build it at the bottom of a hill, and roll, run, or slide down in a box.

TUG-OF-WAR — Pull and tug over a leaf pile; the losers wind up in the leaves.

LEAF RELAY — Divide into teams. Pick two points to run back and forth to. Line up.

The first person on each team starts out with approximately the same amount of leaves held loosely in their arms.

Run to point B, and back to point A trying to hold onto as many leaves as you can. Pass them to the second person on your team. The second person runs back and forth, and passes the leaves to the third person, and so on.

The team that finishes the race first must also have the most leaves left to win.

LEAF BAG HOT POTATO — Fill a plastic bag with leaves. Tie it shut. Throw the bag back and forth for as long as it has leaves in it.

Don't get left holding the bag!

CREEPERS CRAWLERS AND JUMPERS

Have the First Worldwide Worm Race in your backyard or park.

If worms are hard to find, try caterpillars, beetles, or frogs.

Carefully capture your favorite non-biting, non-stinging, friendly crawlies. Set up a race course with a start and finish line. Give each racer a name. Line them up; remember who is who. Bang a pot or pan to start the race. One, two, three, and they're off! If the racers won't start, give them a little helpful push.

Cheer them on.

"NAMING"

We all have a favorite place,
a tree,
a rock,
or a plant.
Do you feel close to it?
Would you miss it if it weren't there?
Then name it.

While you're at it,
give yourself a new name,
one that really says something important about you.
It could be the name of an animal that is a lot like you,
or an object,
or a phrase that describes you.

BIG FOOT'S 100% NATURAL GRAFEET!

In sand or snow,
send a message to a bird, a plane, a satellite,
or visitors from other worlds.

Write very large.

A snowy football field works very well, if
you get there early on a winter morning.

Walk off the letters, one foot in front of
the other, trying to keep your lines straight.

Don't walk between the letters too much,
or your message will be unreadable.

In wet or damp sand, use a large stick to
scratch out the lines of your letters.

SNOWY FOOTBALL FIELD *BEFORE*

AFTER

GROUP STAR GAZE

Gather together with some friends on a clear, dark, warm night.

Find an open space where you can see the sky.

Lie down on a blanket. Arrange yourselves in a circle, heads to the center.

Some Things to Do:

Lie quietly looking at the stars. Don't talk for 15 minutes.

Look for shooting stars.

Spot the Big Dipper.

Imagine what exists beyond the North Star.

Do you think that there is a person on another world lying on a blanket looking up at their night sky, wondering if there is a person on another world lying on a blanket looking up at their night sky...

For those who want to know more:
Check with a local planetarium or a star guide book for easily recognizable sights in the summer night sky. Use a small flashlight and the guide book until you can recognize other constellations, your astrological sign, or a passing satellite.

DISGUISE'S THE LIMIT

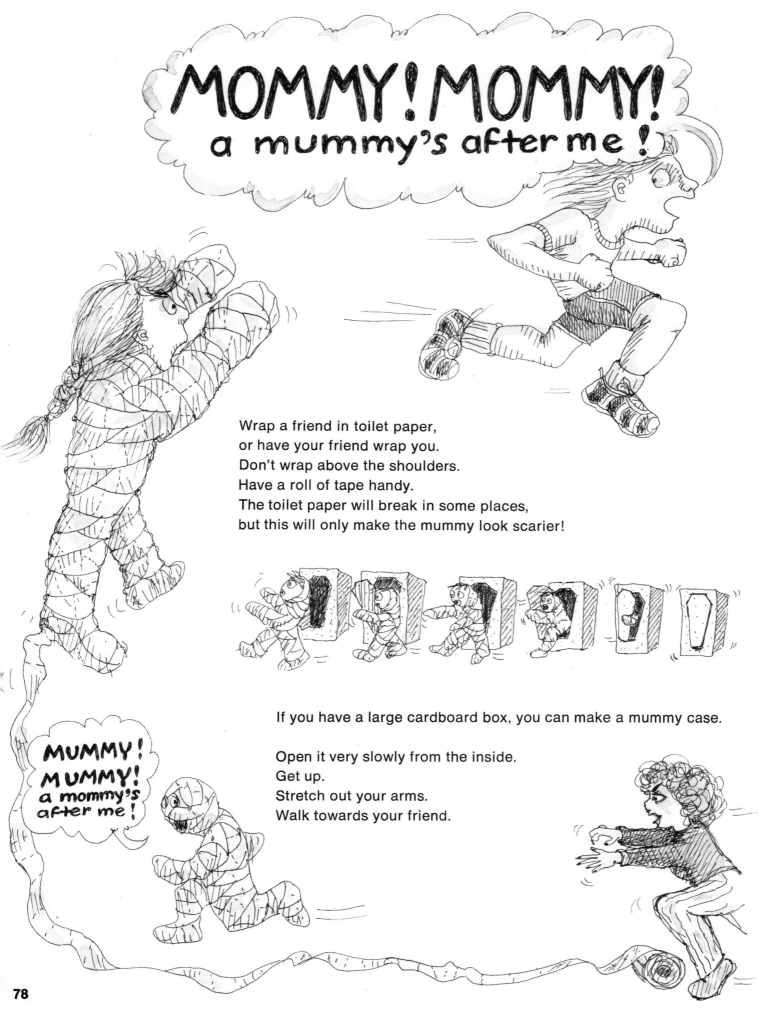

MOMMY! MOMMY!
a mummy's after me!

Wrap a friend in toilet paper,
or have your friend wrap you.
Don't wrap above the shoulders.
Have a roll of tape handy.
The toilet paper will break in some places,
but this will only make the mummy look scarier!

If you have a large cardboard box, you can make a mummy case.

Open it very slowly from the inside.
Get up.
Stretch out your arms.
Walk towards your friend.

MUMMY!
MUMMY!
a mommy's
after me!

GO SOAP YOUR HEAD

On a hot summer day, soak your head.
Lather it up with about twice the amount
of shampoo you usually use.

Stand in front of a mirror
and sculpt your lathered hair, or let
someone else do it.

Make horns, small points, strange curls.
As your hair dries, you might have to reshape
a horn or a point.

When you have the look you want, let it dry.
Put on makeup and a costume to match.

Have someone take a photo of you.

Later rinse your hair out in the tub or shower.

Take a picture of each member of your family, or use old ones that you have permission to cut up.

Make your own funny pictures. You can cut off heads, mix them up, and glue them back on.

Draw comic balloons and write what you want.

Make your own comic strip using a ruler. Paste your family pictures in the boxes. Add your own background and words.

Cut out things from newspapers and magazines that could be pasted onto your pictures: captions, clothes, headlines, products, and scenery.

FAMILY TREE

Have you ever thought about the fact that your family history goes back generations and generations?

See how much of a family tree you can make up.

Ask your mother and father who their parents and grandparents were.

Find out from your parents, grandparents, or other relatives who your great-grandparents were. Keep going as far as you can.

Find out as much as you can about each person on your family tree.

If you want to do more, ask your librarian for some books on genealogy, the study of family history.

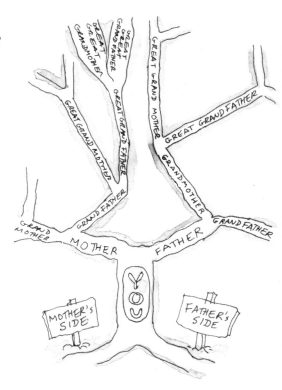

ME by Me

Who are you?
What have you done?
Where have you been?

Write your autobiography.
Seal it in an envelope.

Put it in the time capsule (see page 44), or ask your parent to hold it for ten years.

TELEPHONE-TELEPHONE

Get a group of friends to agree that on a certain day
or evening you will all play Telephone-Telephone.

Set up a phone chain. Tell your friends
which person will call them and
which person they are to call.

You start the chain and have
the last person call you.

Tell a long joke, use a tongue twister,
or make up a story.

Each person is told the story only once,
and must repeat it exactly.

When it gets back to you, write down
what you are told. The next day,
show it to everyone along with
what you originally said.

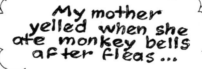

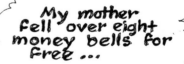

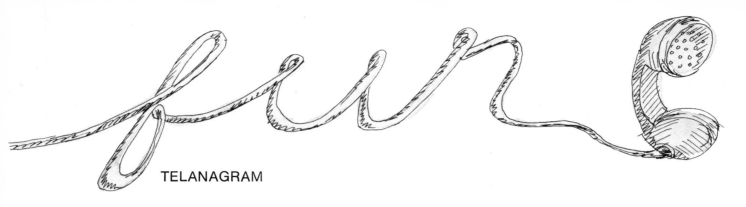

fun

TELANAGRAM

Make a code word from your phone number.

Write your phone number at the top of a piece of paper; spread the numbers out.

Under each number put the letters that correspond on your telephone.

Take only one letter from under each number and try different combinations to make up a whole word.

If you should get stuck, or find a terrific short word, then leave the extra numbers as numbers.

If you need more letters, try using your area code.

2	6	6	5	3	7	7	
abc	mno	mno	lkj	def	prs	prs	◁ Corresponding Letters
b	o	n	k	e	r	s	◁ bonkers
c	o	o	l	e	r	7	◁ cooler 7
a	n	o	k	e	s	p	◁ an o.k. esp
b	o	o	k	3	7	7	◁ book 377

◁ YOUR NUMBER

CAR PHONE

PATCH BEE

Invite a group of friends over.

Ask each to bring: a pair of jeans or a shirt to patch,
a few pieces of fabric,
thread,
needles and pins,
scissors.

Organize a section of floor or table
so that all the supplies can be
placed neatly together.

Your friends add their own
supplies to the common table.

Sit in a circle and share
materials, skills, and conversation.

If there's time, make a few extra patches,
save them, and give them as gifts.

PUTTY FACE

Sit in a circle.

Everyone puts a large paper bag over
his or her head, except for one person.

That person makes the weirdest, funniest face
possible, and taps the next person, who takes off
the paper bag and tries to make the same face.

Pass the face from player to player.

Freeze your face until every face
is showing.

Take turns starting a Putty Face.

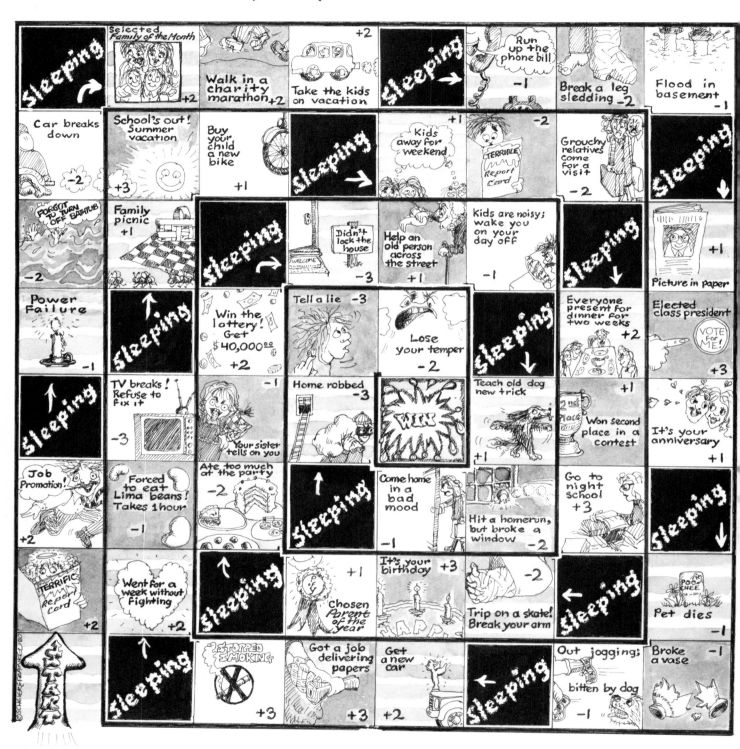

Family NEVER Bored Game

You will need:
a game board, a die, a playing piece for each family member.

RULES:

Everyone rolls the die. Highest number plays first. Object of the game is to travel around the board and be the first to reach the center of the spiral. Follow the instructions on each square if it applies to **you.** A kid who lands on a *parent* square should do nothing that turn. The same rule applies to parents landing on *kid* squares. Both parents and kids should follow the instructions on *family* squares.

If you become stuck in a repeating pattern, advance to nearest *sleeping* square and lose one turn. Alter rules if necessary to suit your particular family.

Rule off 64 squares (8 across and 8 down) on an old board game or on a piece of heavy cardboard, or recycle an old checker board.

Choose four colors of adhesive or construction paper. Make:

16 squares of color #1 for *kids*
16 squares of color #2 for *parents*
15 squares of color #3 for everyone in the *family*
15 squares of color #4 for *sleeping*
1 square at the beginning for *start,*
1 square at the end for *winner.*

As a family group make up 6 lists.
List:

8 good things that could happen to kids
8 bad things that could happen to kids } put these on *kid* squares

8 good things that could happen to parents
8 bad things that could happen to parents } put these on *parent* squares

8 good things that could happen to everyone
7 bad things that could happen to everyone } put these on *family* squares

Assign a value to each good and bad thing.
Good things = 1 to 3 squares ahead (+1 to +3)
Bad things = 1 to 3 squares back (−1 to −3)

Write each item on its color and glue it down in a spiral, alternating every four squares (*kid, parents, sleeping, family*).

Each person chooses a small piece to move around the board: a penny, a plastic charm, a pretty pebble, a cuff link.

DISGUISES

Do your friends' faces.
Have them do yours.

OLD AGE:

You'll need: white highlight makeup pencil
brown eyebrow pencil
baby powder
powder puff or cotton

Draw dark age lines with the brown pencil.
Above each dark line,
draw a white line with the highlight pencil.
Blend each set of two lines together
gently with your finger.
Darken your eyelids.

Follow your own natural lines by wrinkling
your face, frowning, and scowling.

When all the lines are drawn and blended,
powder your face lightly with the baby powder.

Streak powder through your hair to create
gray and white hair.

Remove this makeup with cold cream, soap, and water.
Powder will wash out of hair with shampoo and water.

Use darker makeup pencils for darker skin.

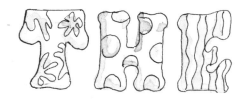 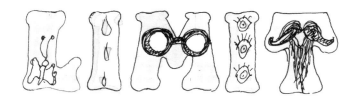

BLOOD, SCABS, AND PIMPLES

Mix syrup and red food coloring,
or mix red or purple jelly and syrup.

Paint on for scars and scabs.

Drip it on,
or drip it from the corner of your mouth.

Dot it on to create pimples and splotches.

PARTS

Use eye makeup pencils, which come in many colors,
to make over your face. Add:

extra eyes

an extra mouth

tape on a pair of glasses
to cover your new pair of eyes

Totally redo yourself.
Shoot a lightning bolt down the middle of your face.
Paint a scene on your forehead.
Make your eyes the centers of two flowers.
Draw on a beard or mustache.
Draw hair all over your hands.

SWAP-IN for PACK RATS

Send out invitations asking your friends to come to your house on a specific day and time, and to bring their old clothes, records, books, junk, or anything else they want to trade.

With your friends spread out the merchandise so everything can be seen.

Wander around and swap.

You might also want to have a

GRAB BAG SPECIAL

Ask each person to bring one thing that's no longer wanted, all wrapped up.

Put all the packages in a pile.

After everyone has arrived, each person picks one package.

WEIGH-IN

Put a bathroom scale in the middle of the room.
Gather around.
Give each person a pencil and paper.

Everyone should list all the players and
write down what they think each person weighs.

One by one your friends or family now
weigh themselves and announce their weight.
Everyone writes the true weights down
next to their guess.

After everyone has weighed in,
figure the difference between each guess and
each real weight. Add up all the differences.
The lowest total wins.

Name	Guess	Real Weight	Difference
MURRAY	145	182	37
JACOB	39	24	15
MILTON	104	130	26
CEIL	121	116	5
		TOTAL ➡	83

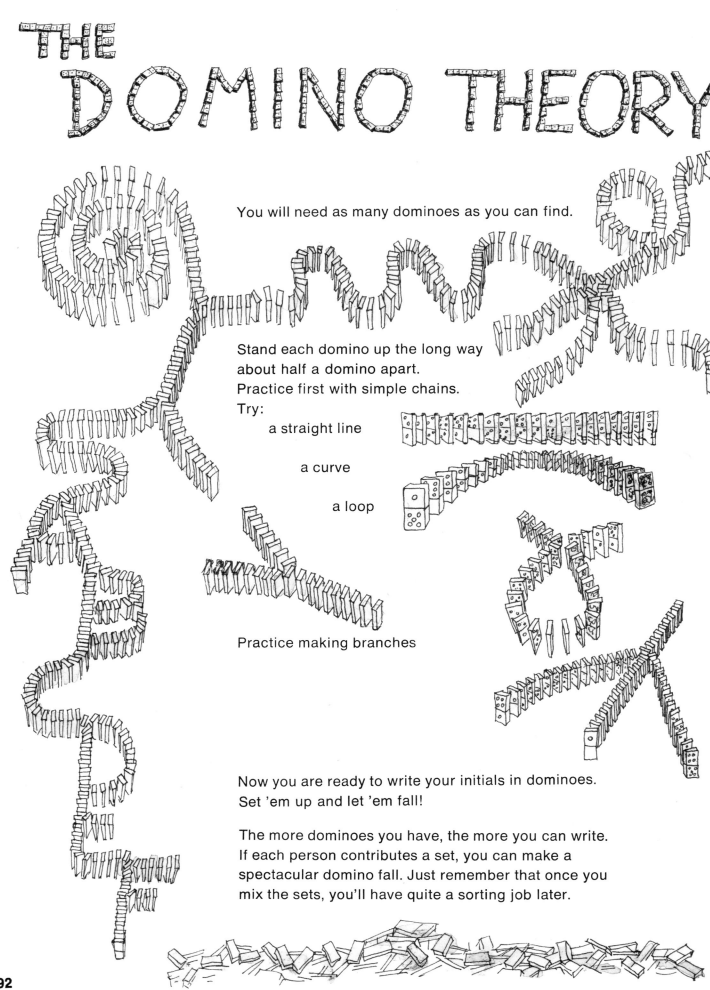

THE DOMINO THEORY

You will need as many dominoes as you can find.

Stand each domino up the long way
about half a domino apart.
Practice first with simple chains.
Try:

      a straight line

        a curve

          a loop

Practice making branches

Now you are ready to write your initials in dominoes.
Set 'em up and let 'em fall!

The more dominoes you have, the more you can write.
If each person contributes a set, you can make a
spectacular domino fall. Just remember that once you
mix the sets, you'll have quite a sorting job later.

GIANT DOMINOES

Make your own set of giant dominoes.

You need 28 large pieces of cardboard.
Save the boards that come with shirts, or
uniformly cut pieces from large boxes.

Draw a line across the middle of each piece.
Then draw the right number of dots.

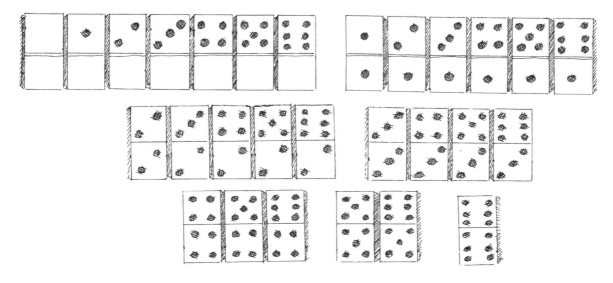

Play in a large space.
Use regular domino rules.

PIN THE PARTS ON THE PRINCIPAL, TAPE THE TOES ON THE TEACHER, OR STICK 5 NOSES ON YOUR SISTER!

Forget that tired old donkey!

On a large piece of brown wrapping paper or cardboard, draw the face of someone it would be fun to stick things on, or use a photograph of that person.

Draw the body without arms or legs.

Draw body parts, or cut them out of magazines. Make extra arms, legs, eyeballs, a beard, mustaches, or horns.

At a party, or with a group of friends, blindfold your guests. Hand them the part they want with tape on it, and steer them in the direction of the body.

ROLES

On a day when everyone in your family
is in a good mood, play roles.

Each person acts out the role
of another family member.

Act as they act.
Talk as they talk.
Eat as they eat.
Walk as they walk.
Say what they say.

THE LAST WORD!

Gather in a circle with one or more people.
Have dictionary, paper, and pencils handy.

The first person opens the dictionary to any page.

Pick a word, any word. One that's weird. One that you like.
One you've never heard of.

Announce your word, spell it, and say what it means.
Everyone writes it down.

Pass the dictionary to the next person, who picks a word.
Do this until you have at least three words, but no
more than ten.

Each person now makes up a silly sentence or story.

There is only one rule:

All the words must be used.

When everyone is finished,
read your stories out loud to each other.